Published in 2023 by Ruby Tuesday Books Ltd.

Copyright © 2023 Ruby Tuesday Books Ltd.

Editor: Mark J. Sachner
Production: John Lingham

Library of Congress Control Number: 2022906047

Print (Hardback) ISBN 978-1-78856-219-5
eBook PDF 978-1-78856-220-1
ePub 978-1-78856-242-3
Published in Minneapolis, MN, USA
Printed in the United States

www.rubytuesdaybooks.com

THE STORY OF OUR TREE

by Ruth Owen

design and illustrations
by Emma Randall

with characters
by Tom Connell

Ruby Tuesday Books

Mr. Hilton wrote the question on the board.

The class had lots of ideas.

This project about trees was going to be lots of FUN!

An acorn

A sweet chestnut tree seed

A horse chestnut tree seed

A leaf changing color

A sycamore tree seed

Everyone brought something into class for the tree project.

A photo of a bird eating berries from a tree

A piece of bark

Oscar had something very special to share with the class.

"I have a letter from our pen pals in Senegal," he said.

With a big smile, Oscar began to read.

Dear Oscar and friends,

This is Fatou! Hello from Senegal. Everyone in our village has been very busy. We are planting trees and we want to tell you all about it . . . .

Fatou

Map of Africa

Sahara Desert

Senegal

Amadou

Awa

Khady

Moussa

Our village is on the edge of the great Sahara Desert.

my home

It is very hot here, and sometimes no rain falls for many months.

Strong winds blow the dry, dusty soil away.

And sometimes, it is difficult to grow enough food.

But our village has a **BIG** plan!

We are growing trees to make the land green again.

Mango trees

Orange trees

Cashew nut trees

Baobab trees

Acacia trees

Acacia tree seed

At school we planted an **acacia tree seed**, and it grew into a seedling.

We planted the little seedling on the edge of our village.

The acacia tree will help our village.

When strong winds blow in from the desert, our tree will shelter us.

The tree will make shade to help cool the hot land.

Grass for our animals will grow in the cool, shady ground.

When rain falls on hot ground, it may dry up quickly. But on cool, shady ground, water has time to trickle down into the soil to the roots of plants.

A tree's roots will cling onto dusty soil and stop it from blowing away.

An acacia tree grows quickly. By the time it is 4 years old, it will be 23 feet (7 meters) tall.

When leaves fall from a tree, they rot on the ground and make new, healthy soil. The new soil contains nutrients that plants need.

Rich, healthy soil soaks up more water than dry, dusty soil.

Our tree will be part of a forest garden on the edge of our village.

Its shade will protect our crops from the hot sun.

When we water our plants, the water will stay in the rich, healthy soil.

Orange tree

Eggplants

Okra

Cabbages

Watermelons

In our forest garden, we will grow food to eat and food to take to the market.

Peppers

Carrots

Potatoes

Onions

Our tree will help everyone breathe.

A tree makes itself a sugary food for energy inside its leaves.

It uses sunlight, water, and a gas from the air called carbon dioxide to do this. This is called photosynthesis.

As trees make their food, they also make oxygen.

We all need oxygen from the air to breathe.

A closed stoma

An open stoma

A leaf has microscopic holes called stomata. Carbon dioxide goes in through the tiny holes, and oxygen comes out.

Every spring, our oak tree will grow new green leaves.

It will also grow male and female flowers.

New leaves

Male flowers

The male flowers release dusty pollen.

The pollen lands here

The acorn grows here

Female flowers

The pollen floats on the breeze and lands on the tiny female flowers.

New acorn

Now the female flowers grow into acorns.

Autumn winds blow the tree's acorns to the ground.

Some acorns settle in the soil and grow into new trees.

But not every one will become a new oak tree.

Blue jay

Blue jays are birds that collect and store acorns to eat in winter. A blue jay may bury up to 5,000 acorns in the ground.

The bird doesn't find all its buried acorns, though, and some grow into trees.

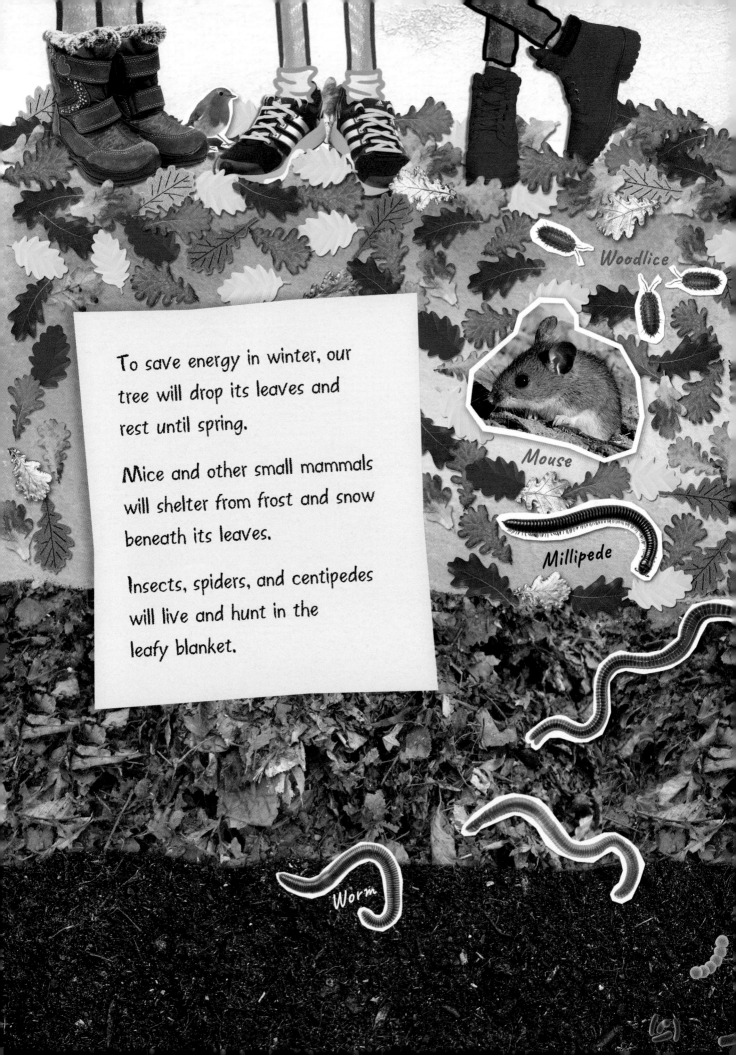

To save energy in winter, our tree will drop its leaves and rest until spring.

Mice and other small mammals will shelter from frost and snow beneath its leaves.

Insects, spiders, and centipedes will live and hunt in the leafy blanket.

Woodlice

Mouse

Millipede

Worm

About 1,000 different kinds of animals will live in our tree!

Bluebird

The tree will become a restaurant for birds! They will visit to eat the insects and spiders that live there.

Robin

Wren

Caterpillar

Twig

Deer feed on moss and bark from the trunks of oak trees.

An oak beauty moth caterpillar munches on oak tree leaves. It's disguised as a twig to hide from birds that want to eat it!

Deer fawn

Owls, woodpeckers, and nuthatches nest in holes in oak trees.

Little owl chicks

Woodpeckers

Nuthatch

Weasel

Eggs →

In winter, hollow branches are cozy shelters for bats.

Pipistrelle bat

Spiders and centipedes hide in tiny cracks in rough bark.

Weasels and snakes climb trees to steal birds' eggs.

Every time Oscar, Fatou, and their friends wrote a letter, they couldn't wait to share the story of their tree.

Dear Fatou and friends,

This is Oscar. Hello from the USA.

Once it's fully grown, our oak tree may produce 150,000 acorns in a single autumn!

The acorns will be an important winter food for squirrels, chipmunks, raccoons—about 100 different kinds of animals.

Oak leaf

Dear Oscar and friends,
This is Fatou. Hello from Senegal.

Acacia leaf

Acacia trees produce a substance called gum acacia.

Gum

The gum dries into hard lumps that can be collected from the tree.

Gum acacia

We will sell the gum from our acacia tree.

It will be used to make candy, chewing gum, and soft drinks.

Our oak tree may live for 1,000 years!

Ancient oak trees are often given names. There are oak trees named Major Oak, Old Knobbley, King of Limbs, and Gog and Magog.

USA to Mars Shuttle

Our acacia tree will help make Africa greener.

Our tree will be part of a Great Green Wall of forests and gardens.

The wall of trees will stretch for 5,000 miles (8,000 km) across Africa.

The Great Green Wall is growing in an area called the Sahel on the edge of the Sahara Desert. People from many different African countries are planting millions of trees in the Sahel.

Sahara Desert

Sahel Region

Our tree will help fight climate change.

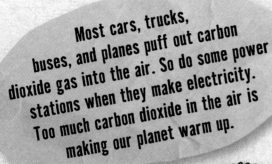

Most cars, trucks, buses, and planes puff out carbon dioxide gas into the air. So do some power stations when they make electricity. Too much carbon dioxide in the air is making our planet warm up.

As our tree makes its food, it will take carbon dioxide out of the air. This will help fight climate change.

Thank you, tree!

Our tree will help fight climate change.

Our tree will take in carbon dioxide, too. Like all trees, it will store the carbon in its wood, keeping it out of the air.

Together, the trees in Africa's Great Green Wall will store millions and millions and millions of tons of carbon.

Thank you, trees!

why are trees important?

We've discovered there are lots of answers to this question.

A tree's dead leaves feed the soil.

Trees cool the land by making shade.

Trees produce oxygen.

Trees make our world more beautiful.

Animals live in trees.

Animals get their food from trees.

Trees help fight climate change.

Trees help make new soil.

Trees store carbon in their wood.

The roots of trees stop dusty soil from blowing away.

Trees produce fruits and other things that people can eat and sell.

When we plant a tree, we do something wonderful for the future.

Would you like to plant a tree, too?

You Can Grow an Oak Tree.

You will need:
- 4 acorns
- Potting soil
- A small trowel
- 5 flowerpots with holes in the bottom about 5 inches (13 cm) tall and 7 inches (18 cm) wide

1: In autumn, collect four acorns. They should be green or brown, and their caps should come off easily. Do not select an acorn that has a hole – this could mean an insect has burrowed inside!

Cap   Acorn

> If you plant four acorns, it gives you four chances to grow a seedling.

2: Put soil into your pot until it is about three-quarters full.

3: Place the 4 acorns on top of the soil with space between each one.

4: Next, cover the acorns with more soil and fill the pot up to about ½ inch (1 cm) from the top.

5: Water the soil so it is moist, and then place the pot outside.

6: In spring, keep watch for tiny shoots. Once your seedlings are growing and roots start to appear out of the bottom of the pot, it's time to repot your seedlings into separate pots so they have more room to grow.

7: Take each pot and half fill it with soil.

8: VERY carefully lay your pot of oak tree seedlings on its side on some grass. Gently tap and tip the pot so that the soil and roots come out, without damaging the leaves and stems of the seedlings.

9: Now, take hold of a seedling by its leaves (not its stem or roots) and place it into a pot. Look at the seedling's stem and note where the soil came up to in the original pot.

10: Carefully add more soil to the pot, up to the level on the seedling's stem that you identified in step 9. Gently pat down the soil.

11: Repeat steps 9 and 10 with the other three seedlings. Water each pot and once again, leave them outside to continue growing.

12: Each of your little oak trees can grow in a pot for two to three years. Or once they are about 10 inches (25 cm) tall, they can be planted in the ground.

> Now you can tell the story of your tree!